I'm not saying, I'm just
saying : a novel

o

p

e

Praise for Matthew Salesses's
I'm Not Saying, I'm Just Saying

"Matthew Salesses' *I'm Not Saying, I'm Not Saying* is an absolute stunner of a novel. Told in short, sharp vignettes with prose that is taut, yet overflowing with meaning, this is the story of a year in the life of a complex and haunted, cobbled together family. The beauty of Salesses' writing here lies in his fearlessness, the emotional blows to the heart and head and gut he's willing to deliver, as if to say: This, this is life! And we are all, in one way or another, survivors."
-Kathy Fish, author of *Together We Can Bury It*

"Matthew Salesses has written an extraordinary and startlingly original novel that explores connection and disconnection, the claims and limitations of the self, and the shifting terrain of truth. Poetic, unforgettable, shot through with fury and yearning, *I'm Not Saying, I'm Just Saying* captures in clear and chilling flashes our capacity for the cruelty and tenderness of love."
-Catherine Chung, author of *Forgotten Country*

"In Matt Salesses's smart novel-in-shorts, a newly-minted father flees telling his own story by any means necessary—by sarcasm, by denial, by playful and precise wordplay—rarely allowing space for his emerging feelings to linger. But the truth of who we might be is not so easily escaped, and it is in the accumulation of many such moments that our narrator, like us, is revealed: both the people we have been, and the better people we might be lucky enough to one day hope to become."
-Matt Bell, author of *In the House upon the Dirt between the Lake and the Woods*

"*I'm Not Saying, I'm Just Saying* renders the messiness of life, family, love in its myriad complex forms—romance lost and found, blood ties, squandered, unrequited—via 115 micro-stories that add up to a pointillist masterpiece."
-Marie Myung-Ok Lee, author of *Somebody's Daughter*

I'm Not Saying, I'm Just Saying

A NOVEL

Matthew Salesses

Also by Matthew Salesses

The Last Repatriate

Our Island of Epidemics

We Will Take What We Can Get

For my wife and daughter

Introduction
by Roxane Gay

Flash fiction is many things, but most readers and writers of the form would agree that flash fiction is, in part, about compression—using few words to tell a story that is not constrained, in scope, by brevity.

Sometimes, though, think of flash fiction as an explosion of a moment, blowing the story of a life wide open, revealing every intimate and ugly detail. An explosion of intimate detail is the best way to describe the very short fictions that comprise Matthew Salesses's *I'm Not Saying, I'm Just Saying*—a novel that is very appealing in its nakedness and emotional honesty, how it reveals one man's flaws and misdeeds as he grapples with a fatherhood he never planned for.

This is not only a novel about fatherhood; it's about love and infidelity and race and loneliness and being lost and working your way toward a found place. In the novel, the narrator has an Asian wifely person and a white girlfriend and an Asian girlfriend and a biracial son he knew nothing about until the mother died, each trying to figure out how to fit into the life of the man who is, for better or worse, at the center of their lives all while he tries to figure out how to rise to his responsibilities, be better to the ones he loves, to simply be better or, perhaps, to simply be.

These 115 very short fictions, these 115 explosive fragments of *I'm Not Saying, I'm Just Saying*, must be considered for the beautiful damage they depict, both as a sum and all parts. Even when these stories are at their most raw, their most garishly intimate, Salesses's writing is so elegant, so moving and intelligent, you cannot look away. The writing will not allow you such mercy. *I'm Not Saying, I'm Just Saying* will not even allow you to want such mercy as the book's power and beauty and truth hold you in thrall.

Contents

I'm Not Saying, I'm Just Saying

The Night I Met Her She Said Once You Go Yellow

The boy I still wasn't sure was mine stared at the wash of starfish stinking on the sand and said something boyish about the ocean being big and cruel. I tried to tell him the starfish weren't all dead yet, but he knew enough already to tell the difference. So I lied more. I told him that starfish were even better than lizards, that if you broke off a dead piece of them it grew back alive. His mother, a one-night stand, had told him about lizards. She'd gotten it into his head that this was what he should tell the man he thought was his father—she had a keen sense of metaphor, was all I remembered about her, which was enough. The ocean washed over the starfish and they twinkled with deadness. The boy rushed against the wake and plucked one out of the surf and I noticed his black hair curl at its ends like mine. He brought the starfish back, stiff as a bad joke. He snapped off a leg, and I could see on his half-white face that he'd overestimated both how mean and how hopeful he'd thought he could be. Don't worry, I thought, those feelings will come.

19

Gifts

I pitied the boy for believing in me, but maybe that wasn't why I let him see where I lived. A dead bird waited on the stoop, blue with a natural unnaturalness. When we got inside, I remembered I had the girl over, the one who might have looked like his mother: the white one, I mean. She'd been asleep when I left that morning. I'd thought maybe she would figure things out on her own. But she wasn't the sharpest, etc. The boy stood in the doorway as if unsure whether he was invited in. I thought his mom was dead, so his manners surprised me. He stared at the bird. The white girl heard his crying and came downstairs. "It's okay, baby," she said. I saw she had thought it was me. I almost said, "This isn't going to work." Then I realized maybe I'd brought the boy to scare her. I stared at his half-Korean neck. "The cat left that," I told him. "It's a gift. When an animal loves you, it kills something for you." I didn't see how those words might come back to bite me.

20

I Wasn't Planning on Calling Anyone Back

After I made the girl who was not his mother leave, the boy told me he wanted to draw me a picture. I got ready for lip, but he meant literally. I gave him a piece of paper that said, "I'll stay wet," on the other side. I thought it was going to be one of those moments, like in a scary movie with a scary devil child. But the boy drew a woman in bed with a cross behind her on the wall. "Was that your mom?" I asked. He said, "Is." I didn't realize he was old enough to have a sense of tense; he was five. I said, "Don't start to cry again." He drew on his arm. "*We* were a family," he said like asking. But we never were. On his arm was another cross. I asked which hospital she was in. The thing about him and his innocence that almost broke my heart: it took him a double-take to figure out how I knew where she was. "Can I draw you another picture?" he said, thinking he'd missed something.

Bad Habits

When it got late, the boy could guess I would make him leave soon. I was as alone with my drink as I always was. He tapped the glass with a dirty fingernail. Then he studied the fingernail and heaved a series of sighs. I covered my drink. I didn't want to see what would come out of him. I figured his fingernails were too long so he was thinking about his mom, who usually cut them. I didn't know where the clippers were; I had always bit my nails to the skin.

22

Nullius Filius Is Not a Pun

The wifely woman came back fresh as a schoolgirl, licking a candy cane in summer, in love again by our absence. She was so unprepared for what I was about to lay on her. We'd never wanted kids. I hadn't seen her in weeks and I was sick of the women who weren't her. In bed, I tried to convince her I'd missed her and instead convinced myself she saw through me. I was scared of losing her was why I gave her such reasons to leave. I didn't want to wonder, when eventually she disappeared, whether it was because she just didn't love me. She rolled the cane on my skin and left faint red stripes. I wondered why the white didn't come off. She licked the stripes and put the cane where she wanted on herself. After I came, she said, "The bad news first." I could see her x-raying through to my fears. She always wanted the good news last; I wondered what to tell her.

Reflection Is as Reflection Does

As I broke the news of the boy, she sat stunned in the din of ex-girlfriends. I could see her working out which was the mom, from my half-truths. All I could recall of that woman were words, the unfortunate turns of phrase: "just slip it in," to the question of protection. I hadn't told the wifely woman everything about my past. Some things I didn't know, clearly. Occasionally the truth would reveal itself to her before me, as if it knew all along to whom it should belong. I said she should look in the boy's face to guess the second helix. Later, they would stare into the mirror together, crossing paths.

24

The Meaning of Numbers

The wifely woman and I went to the hospital where the half-white boy's mother was waiting to confirm me as his father. I was waiting to compare this object of my past desire to the object of my desire now. I couldn't honestly remember her. Maybe, I thought at first, she wouldn't remember me either—but she'd had five years to blame me. I'd only known the boy a week. I figured she'd been dying for a week. In the hospital room, death seemed cherished, not rushed. She tapped what looked like a calculator, as if calculating her end date. The wifely woman glared at me like she didn't know what to think of *herself*, anymore, if this was the type of girl I made babies with. The boy climbed onto the bed and took the symbol from his mother and gave it to me. I typed out *HELL* upside-down: seven seven three four. "You forgot the *0*," the boy said. The wifely woman said, "So you know this game."

I Guess That Meant We Looked Like Life

In the hospital, people smiled at the boy and then looked sadly at us and turned away. After a few such encounters with pity, the wifely woman hissed in my ear, "I think they think *he's* the one dying." The boy looked like death, both harbinger and sentenced. It had rubbed off on him from his mom. His mom had a body I couldn't recall even confronted with her mortality. In the hall, the wifely woman and I held a hand of his each, swinging him when he lifted his feet. She knelt and straightened his hair as if the roots of his problems grew in his head. He watched her mothering with his mom in his eyes. I sneered until we got out of there, to make sure people knew we were all the same, we three.

Not Just a Drinking Game

I slipped away from the past and the soon-to-be-past to find somewhere dirty to cleanse myself. I woke in the cupped hands of alcohol, unsure where I'd been. In the morning shadows, a bar stretched and contracted. In my hand shone a quarter. The wifely woman looked ravaged, as in *ravaged*—at least I'd remembered my destination. "You won and you lost," the wifely woman said without rising, illuminating nothing. The quarter left a scarlet circle on my palm. I wondered if the circle cousined her scorn. "Did you find what you wanted?" she asked. I hoped I'd needed those twenty-five cents. I hoped they'd meant something.

Circumnavigation

When the white girl was over, she liked to explore where I lived. She wore the wifely woman's slippers with her own gel inserts. A gel my company did the ads for. She'd found the ads on a worst-of list and connected me to them through intuition or internet. I refused to discuss work. The rhymes signaled in my head like flags: she put the gel in Magellan. I hated her imperial stride.

Nothing to the Imagination

The wifely woman and I went to a movie to imagine something far from a real child. I'd always hated child actors too young to fake it. The wifely woman liked their innocence unable to hide. This time, we saw a flick with a cop and a robber. It was hard to tell who was the good guy, but it was important to know, or at least guess. "Why is there so much nudity in violent movies?" the wifely woman said. I said, "You did say nudity?"

More Games

We had a while to decide hide or seek. The boy, I assumed, slept over in the hospital. I guessed he didn't have a step-dad? I guessed his mom was holding onto more than hope? My history was crock-full of overestimating myself. That's how I'd always kept ahead of life. The wifely woman had come back from business and meant business. I feared that part of her that could execute Powerpoint. How to graph the boy, I wondered—I'd never made a winning presentation. The last game of hide and seek I played, I was still lost.

30

TV Was a Friend and an Enemy

After his mother passed, the boy who claimed he was mine became addicted to tragedy. The wifely woman said we had no choice, but I think she was happy to let him stay with us. She said the choice thing for my benefit. The boy liked to watch the *obits*. That was what the news had become since they'd started competing with Fox. The boy didn't know what *obits* meant; he just liked to watch death in general. It was what his mother and he had watched in the hospital. I understood: she'd wanted to know she was not alone. It was normal to "know" things you couldn't. The boy would relate the worst deaths to the wifely woman and me over dinner. Try drinking anything as a five-year-old says a woman bled to death after reaching into a garbage disposal. This was the class of death his mother had had to compete with. "You want to adopt that?" I said when the boy said a man had tried to lawn mow his brother's back hair. The wifely woman said, "Don't say the a-word." I didn't think the boy knew what I meant, but it was true he was a genius at context.

31

Isn't This How That Works?
For Grace Paley

On the beach, someone stapled pages, never out of his box. I hated to be reminded that I was on vacation, not life. At work, I worked on other people's wants: bodies, mostly. I wanted a body, too, of course. But more so, I wanted something less sellable. The stapler on the beach set me off. I wanted to burn away or burn up in life. I wanted my wants to have nothing to do with anyone else's. Now, as if in another life, a boy owned me. I kept watch over him in the waves. I tried to think: vacation, or paternity.

I Tell You This Is Irony

I showed up to work, finally, with a heavy head and a briefcase full of drugs that would float me like a balloon when I gave up working, co-pay on the drugs thanks to the wifely woman. I had nothing of my own. The day started dead-end out of the driveway. Dumbo ears was next to me; that was new. I looked around but there was my dying ficus, still dying. The stapler said my name on it, which I'd done ironically. In my office, no one noticed irony. Dumbo ears said, "I thought you got fired." I said, "You keeping track of my hours?" I said, "I've got problems you only see in Korean melodramas." I said, "Want to fight?" Maybe I wouldn't need the drugs after all, I thought, if I could get that lightness throwing punches. His jaw clicked, but he only smoothed down his puckered tie. I stapled my hand to the desk, vaguely aware that things were getting fuzzy around the edges. He tucked his chin into his collar. A few minutes later, I realized I *hadn't* shown him. When I pulled the staple out, I had the world's least impressive vampire bite.

She Was a Tsunami to His Earthquake

I noticed my life shaken. The wifely woman had accepted my bastard, but this was not disaster. She said analogies would get me nowhere. I had zero response. I didn't know where I stood on acceptance. I self-medicated. I sent bottles drifting out into a sea of garbage. The earth never answered. I thought, destruction is nothing. The wifely woman recycled. The boy asked what was made with all that plastic, and I said, more plastic.

More Than a Distraction

I had to blow off some steam, and the white girl had been sending texts I barely had time to delete. I had another girl, too, but she was Asian like us and I thought the wifely woman knew about her. So I met the white girl in her apartment. "Who was that kid the other day?" she said after we'd fooled around a little but not enough. I tried with a half-coddled heart to forget I might have a son. He was just a boy; I remembered my own boyhood. Boys had nothing better to do than to hold onto their dreams with what they didn't yet realize was desperation. The white girl said she didn't know why women liked me—a mystery, I agreed. I almost considered talking. She could have used someone to talk to.

The Boy Was the One with the Territory Issues

I gave the wifely woman a sunflower, which soon drooped in its vase, broken. We had a cat and a boy who might be my son, candidates for passive aggression. Since the boy arrived, the cat had left scratches on his backpack, a hairball in his sneaker. But it didn't object to a little petting. The boy tried to over-love it, which—a lesson—had backfired. I wondered if the boy was really learning. I caught him watering the snapped flower.

Everyone's Playing His Trump Card

In her wisdom, the wifely woman strategized the social worker's entire visit. She laid it out like a game of Risk, which the boy liked and pretended he understood. "He's *your* son," she said, meaning why didn't *I* plan? I put my mouth to her ear so I could whisper, "Supposedly." I told the boy to hold a glass of milk, to sip it when he felt nervous—it was a trick my father had taught me. I said, "We'll play the good parents giving the boy his calcium." I told the boy, "This will make your bones invincible." The boy was still in his tragic phase, repeating deaths from the news. This was likely what had the wifely woman so worried, that we would look like we couldn't fill the loss of his real mother; of course, I thought, *that death* was why anyone cared about us. The boy said, "Dan Rather said." I told him to shut up about Dan Rather in public. I poured him the glass of milk. The social worker was a short brunette who would have been attractive if she hadn't been a social worker; it was something about her eyes, which were everywhere. She studied our predictable apartment like it was about to confess a murder. The boy followed her around and I worried that the social worker would think he was conflating her with his mother. He said, "A

boy at a circus in Indiana made the clowns call 911 but couldn't save his mom's life." I thought, not so on the nose, kid. He said, "I have a glass of milk my dad gave me." The wifely woman pulled his pants higher and blushed. He was five. I watched to see if my father's trick was worth anything. The social worker said, "That's a beer mug, not a glass." She ordered some tests done. From the way the boy was holding the beer mug, I already knew they'd be positive.

And Yet Girls Can Fool Themselves

During my lunch break, I went to bother my therapist. A surprise visit—I liked to sneak-attack her. She was on lunch, too, but I knew she ate in her office. Her one little slip, besides, or in combination with, sleeping with me. She wouldn't open the door until I told her it was an emergency, I'd developed a responsibility. When she let me inside and asked her question, I said, "I said 'a.' " I said, "Still, I may be a father." I explained the half-white boy's claim on my past, the chain from sex to my future. Me and commitment she knew two ways over. "So what can I do?" I asked. She said, "I don't give advice, remember. I'm a therapist?" I reminded her of the session I hadn't paid for. She said, "I could slap you, for both me and the boy. But would that make a difference?"

39

The Old Language Was Dead

The Xanax kept me so close I couldn't tell if I was its friend or enemy. Work battled away in the background. I stared at my telephone, feeling calm. Well, I thought, ring. I didn't have a project worth calling for, only a set of slogans. I made simple romance, whoring out words that wouldn't marry. For a furniture line, I wrote, "Cushioning blows." I wrote, "If you love sofas, a love sofa." I was out of practice. I imagined love on the love sofa. I snuggled with the drugs. In the morning, I had driven the boy to his blood tests. I wrote, "A Lazyboy by any other name." But the boss had a moratorium on Shakespeare. I read the label in my hand: "Three times daily." I waited for the phone to ring. I wrote, "Home is where the love sofa is." I wrote, "The way to a man's love sofa is through his stomach." But that was missing the point. I had to stop writing prescriptions.

40

The Girl Was Saved in My Phone as "For Emergencies"

After a day of inappropriate urges, I called the side girl-on-the-side. She didn't know anything about the boy and the positive blood test. She didn't know anything about anything. She wasn't pretty except to white boys, and she was the type who would never marry anyone who wasn't Asian and would never sleep with anyone she would never marry. I had to be careful with her, though I wasn't technically married, because she collected the crumbs of truth, but for an hour with her, I was someone else, and when I left, I could discard that part of me and know it would be repossessed.

Since We Were Both Asian

Once we woke from our aches, I asked her what she would think if she had a mixed baby, and she said, "That I was raped." My response was no response. I didn't want her to know I was choking on fatherhood, Heimliching myself with sex that meant and made nothing.

42

The Purple Heart Marines

So I accepted the boy as mine; who was I to stand in the way of hard proof? And about a week afterward, a parade marched through our little suburb, and I took the boy to see it because he was still getting over his mother's death, though he had stopped following the deaths on the news. Other deaths no longer comforted him. Occasionally, a stray tragedy he'd memorized would still pop out—I would be washing the cat's bowl and he would say a man drowned in a river in Iowa after dropping his umbrella in the water. He would say the umbrella opened up as the man reached for it and the man just swept downstream. But mostly, he kept quiet. I didn't want to believe these tragedies, but when I searched for them online, there they were, filed under "strange news" or "Darwin awards." During the parade, the boy said he thought he could be happy soon, in response to nothing; I had never said a word. He was just offering this up, as if *I* were the one who needed to hear it. A veteran marched by and saw the boy's tears. He took off his hat, set it on the boy's head and said, "Soldier." Still I had said nothing.

43

My Life Was Always Drunk Dialing Me

Midday the wifely woman called me at work and said, "Here's the thing about working." We ran out together for drinks. We drank until we knew our jobs would barely suffer us, and then we returned to work and texted. I got sloppy, but I sent the text to her about a sexier girl in the ad before I sent the email to the big boss about real sex. My wires were always crossing. I got a message back from the wifely woman to get my job off my mind. I texted her: which of these me's did she want to survive, because one of us wasn't going to make it?

44

The State of Consumerism

Work was a joke with no punch line. Sometimes, for shits, I would pretend Dumbo ears was a friend. I asked him about foosball, and when he mentioned the Niners, I said, "I said foosball." The company cut off our computers to games, trying to make the internet humorless. But how did they think we were going to sell anything, if we couldn't laugh as we played ourselves?

45

A World Without Legos

Rain rolled in and on the TV we stormed the castle. We swung our controllers like hands. Soon the wifely woman gave up to watch the gloom *outside*. I thought the boy would continue to play—what else were boys for?—but he joined her. I killed the king. The game gave the option to spare the queen, but I wanted the level to end faster. I felt the growing mood. In the game, the rain could wash the dead from their graves. I had seen this secret the day before and meant to keep it from the boy. But I could see now he already knew about rain. He didn't mention his mom; he only stood there and took the wifely woman's hand and let the real rain lure silence. Yet the wifely woman drew him close, as if under an umbrella, and apologized for our unguarded lives.

Good Thing She Had Money

The wifely woman borrowed her old bed—her parents had
kept it decadeless, not such a surprise for Asian parents—
and the first thing the boy did was wet the mattress pad as
if contesting the territory. "It's okay," we both said, getting
ahead of each other with sympathy. I felt impressed by his
sense of ownership. The wifely woman thought he feared
sleeping there because of her, as if a night's rest in her history would make him forget his mother. Though maybe it
was the scent of moths and mothballs, maybe it was more
animal. We let him pee on our bed, to show it didn't matter, not such a surprise for Asian parents.

47

A Ban on Saturday Mornings

The boy called the cat Tom, though I'm almost sure he knew the difference. It was because of the cartoon. We had called the cat Jerry, big mistake, though we hadn't expected a five-year-old then. The cat was all we thought we would ever adopt. The cat couldn't understand us, so it got off scot free. The wifely woman, I could see, was starting to love the boy more. I hit the boy for yanking the cat's tail. But the cat often forgot the tail was a part of it; maybe the boy thought it needed reminding. I told him I didn't want a tail without a cat—what would I do with *that* riddle?

48

She Was Digestive to a Tract

Did it matter if the wifely woman loved the boy because of me? When she made up her mind to love you, she swallowed you whole. Hers was love as intestinal fortitude. I had always wanted to be digested (I had wanted someone who understood how to break me down)—but the boy? After his last visit, he had stayed in the window glass, a fading breath, and she had kept him there. Each day, she had breathed in the same spot. It wasn't clear what the force was that acted on us.

What Do You Want, a Cookie?

The white girl always prepared something to set us afloat. She baked goods out of drugs, surprising from how clean her hair smelled. I met her after work and she stuffed a cookie in my mouth and pumped my jaw like a well handle. Soon this was funny, as if we were wasting water in a draught. "You're so stingy with your love," she said, her laughter not coming off. I insisted "Puff, puff, pass." I sprawled on her floor and texted the wifely woman about a beer with a friend. She texted back that she and the boy were finding old photos of me with the beard I'd abandoned. She had a way with words. "Be here," the white girl said, "at least when you're here." I was nowhere. The river was rushing beneath us. I tilted my chin, testing for thirst.

Life's Groceries

It wasn't all sunshine and moonbeams, is what I mean.
The things we never had to do for the boy:

- Birth him
- Cut his umbilical
- Breastfeed
- Burp him
- Change his diapers
- Babyproof
- Potty-train
- Teach him to swim
- Hit him

You'll notice nowhere in that list is regret.

Women Like Clean

The big boss handed down a project to me personally, and I got the feeling it was a last chance. The product was hand sanitizer. I used it twice an hour, wondering how to sell it. All I could think was, scare tactics. The flu had taken on animal modifiers. I drew up the hand sanitizer as a lupus keeping away a swine and an avian. I drew up the hand sanitizer as a guard dog. Where was my humanity? The wifely woman had made it clear I couldn't quit, not with the boy, before I even stated my case. She earned enough for all of us, but she was only wifely, not wife, so she and the boy had zero technical ties. I didn't say she loved him more, because we had the argument in front of him. He wanted to help, I could tell, but what did he know about hand sanitizer? I had noticed the dirt in his mother's nails before she died; that's not even a metaphor. I touched the wifely woman's nose. I said, "Smell my hands. Is this the kind of man you wanted?" Then I got an idea to make everyone happy.

The Dying Season

As the cold wrestled autumn to submission, we thought about pumpkins. Even the office turned orange—after all, holidays made holiday money. The wifely woman always ogled costumes, but a child jack-o-lantern took the pie. The boy jumped at anything that gained him attention. They were both so overeager, he and she, challenging their associations. I wondered how the boy avoided thoughts of endings. In past years, the wifely woman had worn young and slutty.

What's the Opposite of Succubus?

The Asian girl was a graphic designer. I stole her ideas when I could. She said she gave them to me. She had a thing about gifts. You couldn't take anything from her. That was what frustrated me; she made everything I stole seem a favor. Maybe I came back to her because I wanted her to see her delusion; then I liked the delusion—it suited me. She thought it suited me that she was Asian, she didn't know I had an Asian girl at home. I lied about everything, to see how far I could get. She must know, I often told myself, the telling a favor to us both.

Now Asians Were Cats

I looked at her knuckled back and almost thought about taking care of her. I said, "What are you doing with me?" or maybe she said it. She said, "How long can you stay?" Sometimes, as I thought of our similar upbringing, I wondered if she preferred the lies. Adultery was one thing, tiger parenting another, but maybe I was begging the question. I detested *tiger* to explain the vicious love by which our parents held us in their mouths. The Asian girl, when I was with her those few hours per month, was always short on love. After I left, she was short on vicious. I was the opposite. I liked to cuddle my lies as close as limbs. She lay pressed to me, half-revealed. I touched her dimple and said it was time to go, and she meowed.

The Trick of Advertising

The big boss came round to my cube and bestowed his hand like a crown. He said I'd earned my paycheck for once: making men more womanly, for women, now that was an idea to set the sexes at war. He was always equating war with sex. The numbers didn't lie—people left the screen tests sniffing their palms. Hand lotion was war. Sometimes the women would smell the men, proving some point about selling ourselves.

Biological Clocks

The wifely woman did things I was almost sure she'd said she would never do again. I didn't remind her. I didn't remind her of Hawaii when she'd held herself open and said "lei-ed." I didn't remind her of her curiosity for shaming porn. I didn't remind her of mine. Maybe she didn't remember we'd done these things before—I tried to stop over-thinking. I was memorable. We had a kid in the house now, and maybe she didn't want to be reminded. Just shut up, I thought to my thoughts.

Asians Didn't Plant Apples

The question of the boy had zero answers, but it never stopped asking. Such is life, I said when the boy asked how long it would take me to love him. I wasn't completely cruel—this was a conversation of stares, a lesson of clinging to pant legs, nothing aloud. When we talked, the boy talked about death and I talked about the living living, like that cliché might fit into the lock he'd forged. He wore the wifely woman's favorite pot on his head, and I recalled Johnny Appleseed, my childhood wish to sow America. He was only shielding himself, but I played along, waiting for growth to grow in his wake.

Arts and Crafts

The wifely woman and I taught the boy to make ice cream. I had learned in school and never gotten over the salt. The ice cream you could make in the Dead Sea, I had thought. I didn't mention this to the boy because what if he didn't get the difference between a place and death. He'd just stopped talking about his mom as in a *location*. The wifely woman and I made competing vanillas, shaking the cans until our arms hurt. The boy taste-tested. I imagined a prize for losing. But what he liked best was Fudgesicles. He had a cheap tongue he was only learning to wield, which wasn't from me. I didn't mention his mom. The next day, the wifely woman brought home a box of Fudgesicles and we used the sticks to make something we could unmake.

We Were Not Always Like This

I went out with the boys to celebrate saving my worthless job. The boys were in a rare state, sloshing on each other with gusto. During the third round, brass knuckles appeared on the bar, courtesy of Randy, my closest friend and the most disconnected from reality. Maybe we were all on board for a fight as soon as we saw those knuckles, a symbol of our angry youths before the burbs. We were the boys because we were the boys who had made it: rural and urban weak but suburban strutters. Randy eyed a group of pretenders and flashed his brass. The cops came so quickly we hardly earned the cuffs. Later, in the station, Randy cried, on the hook for his weapon of minor destruction. I tried to be sorry, too. Yet I felt only wonder at our idea of pleasure. "Bring the boy," I said on the phone, sensing a lesson in testosterone. The wifely woman brought only make-up. A black eye was a matter of Shu Uemura to her. I wondered how much we could hide from each other if we wanted it mutually.

What Not to Do with a Bastard Child

The boy heard I had been in the slammer, but there were
worse things for him to hate me for. I said, "Your mom
would roll over in her grave," as I showed him the scrapes
on my wrists. Ever the bomb dog for subtext, he gazed
at the wifely woman. I said, "I didn't mean it that way."
I said, "Yes, she's your mom now." I tried to tell him
I didn't speak in double meanings. But he knew how I
watched him sometimes. I had seen his mother naked,
one night, and now here he was, a mash-up of my current
life and a life I didn't remember, or want to.

Negatives

The boy had grandparents on his mom's side, sure, but I wasn't about to see them. They hadn't claimed him after her funeral, and I didn't want to get involved with that level of devotion. They must have had lives they did cling to; the boy, I guessed, wasn't dead enough. They had their daughter's gravestone. The boy never asked to see the cemetery. I never offered to run into anyone. Maybe he forgot I had parents, or maybe he didn't.

Three Blind Etc.

My mother sent me some Asian chain email before lunch with a list of bullet points praising Korean moms. She always did this, voted her choice of topics; Dad had let slip that she didn't trust my civility anymore. I had accused her (*one* time) of thieving my childhood, forty-five minutes after she brought up my love life. The things she said would crawl into my invisible spaces, you see, like mice, waiting for a crumb to drop. Our problem was she didn't connect what I said later with what she said earlier. I didn't say it right away because I loved her. Over lunch this time, after the *blah blah* about Korean moms, it was a complaint against the wifely woman. Even Dad chimed in: "She's just Chinese." I'd almost forgotten he was there until that "just." "Close enough," I said to piss them off. The entire time, they had ignored what I'd said about having a son I didn't know I had. Dad had gotten drunk. At the end of the meal, Mom mumbled, "A bastard child." You see where I got my mice.

She Combed His Hair

The wifely woman and I always talked about our parents like a warning; what happened to me could happen to you, too. Our families were always one-upping each other's crazy. But this time, the wifely woman said, "They worry." She never defended my mother; we'd even given her her own superhero name, The Eroder, as in confidence, to go with her superpower. Suddenly she was supposed to be The Grandma. The wifely woman said, "Don't you understand, a little?" I wanted her to clarify, understand her or my parents, but I could see my shaky footing getting shakier. Later, the wifely woman stood by the sleeping kid and said, "He's your bastard, why do I care more about him than you do?"

I Told the Boy the Gloves Wanted to Be Together

We got a babysitter for the boy. It was the first time the wifely woman and I had been able to go out for a while. I was cheating on her but didn't want to. She had bailed me out of jail. I wanted this date to prove something. I'd made a reservation at the Coliseum of restaurants. People battled their food for survival and we laughed about the murder faces they made before they let their salads have it. She stole a cloth napkin for her Scrap Book of Our Happiness. Out in the cold, she bundled against me, and I didn't mention she'd lost a glove; I wanted her skin. She didn't mention it either. Then later she sewed a replacement from the napkin, saving the shreds, so she had two mismatching gloves that somehow matched. When the boy saw, he wanted the same, but I wouldn't let him throw out the pair he already owned.

65

It Looked Like a Vibrator

I watched the boy play with the cat, in and out of a box. I had another assignment for work and I thought, kids and pets will go gaga! My product slumped in the corner, less interesting than its container. I thought, a break from kids and pets, no one will try to steal it! How could I sell what a kid couldn't see as potential? I had to think: what was missing from innocence? The wifely woman came home and I recalled when she used to take off her clothes as she entered. Maybe I'd glimpsed an end of "selling it."

When You Look into the Sun, You See Its Shadow for a Moment Afterward

I remembered the day I'd asked her to marry me. I had planned nothing; I hurt with her so much it hurt. She shut her eyes and my lungs blistered. I thought *engagement* with one hot breath. When I stopped talking, she shook her head without opening her eyes. She didn't cut me off, at least. She said, "When I look up, go back in time." I said, "Go forward." We did both, we thought.

We Didn't Know Much About Children

I took the boy to the park wrapped in the wifely woman's idea of warmth. He barely had room to shiver. The other kids played open-necked until they steamed. There was a half hour before the sun went down, and the boy believed in efficiency; his mother, death, etc. We'd accepted his lacks since we knew that half the genes were mine. We knew little about his mom. Sometimes I could see my dad in his disappointment.

Foreplay

Just when I needed it, the white girl slipped the hairband around my two wrists and let her hair lick my chest. For an hour, she had been using the band as a prop. I had been thinking about the boy's thick look as I dropped him at his new kindergarten. The boy and I had an understanding. His permanence wasn't exactly permanence. The white girl and I had the same understanding. No one would talk. I could bust out of the band but I stayed put, all about pretend. Then in the corner yawned yellow eyes. The white girl's lips brushed goose bumps, and it took me a minute to ID the glow. "You got a cat," I said. She said, "You have a cat and a son." I tried to remember to pull away before a hickey. I winged my elbows out and the band sprang across the room, the cat springing after it. The white girl pulled down her lips with two fingers to be sure of her frown. I wasn't expecting it when the cat fetched back the band like a poodle. "You got a dog," I said as she rebound my wrists.

She Said "My Idea" Like It Belonged to Her

The white girl skipped over a month of half-whispers and got loud. She said she got the cat because of me, did I know that. She said did I know about litter boxes. She said that's how I treated her, like she would scoop up what I had buried. I wasn't purring when she sprawled on her bed, but I wasn't the animal she said I was. I didn't defend myself. I was done with comparisons. I waited for her to get to who I was.

70

The Wifely Woman Won the Bet

The boy was cutest when he was asleep, not being his own worst enemy, not comparing us to his mother. We watched his lips curl, his arms shudder. When his breaths deepened, I wanted to bet on his dreams. Asleep, he was more expressive of fears and desires. The wifely woman bet happiness, of course—*or*, she said, escapism. I bet on his toughness, a furrowed brow. I bet he couldn't get away from who he was. He blew out his cheeks and flapped his arms like a drowner. She shook him awake. He said he dreamed he could fly if he held his breath, which had us puzzled for metaphor.

71

If You Give a Mouse a Marshmallow

The wifely woman believed in the power of future ice creams, but I could see the boy keeping count. One day he would collect, I thought, and we'd be out a boy or twenty-seven ice creams. I knew the number, too, because I was nervous. I was nervous the boy would ask me how many, and I would want to tell the truth. The wifely woman said she had seen a study about delayed gratification; she said the kids who could wait would grow up into success. She showed me the video on YouTube. One girl picked a hole in her marshmallow, ate the middle, and sealed it back up. That was the girl I had my money on. We argued until I looked down and the boy was gone—I panicked, though I'd said I wanted this moment to come. The wifely woman didn't rub it in; she knew exactly where he was, which was enough.

If Only We Knew What That Was

I begged a night out for Randy's sake, whom I hadn't seen since jail. He had broken down and now denied it, but you could see the trace of arrest in how he rubbed his wrists. He'd adopted a German shepherd and we took it for a walk. It dropped its head on the bar like a drunk. Randy argued with the bartender, saying the dog had been a seeing-eye and didn't like to separate. I said we were teaching it the trick of being human. The bartender relented after they shook paws—the dog, at least, knew how to close a deal. Afterward, Randy told me it had bit its blind person; that's why he had chosen it. It had gotten fed up with always having to lead.

I Had Always Avoided a Nickname

With the rumor that the little boss was about to quit, I got ambition at last. I'd made the least of my job for so long that maybe it was just odds. Dumbo ears was next in line, but we didn't call him Dumbo ears because of his ears—that was subterfuge. I knew the big boss liked to boss drunk; he was always saying he *could have been* an alcoholic. So I used the wifely woman's money to buy an ancient scotch. I wasn't the best at drawing up ads, that was true, but I could be a politician, and the little boss had to be a politician. The big boss drank himself generous and I used his hangover to convince him his drunkenness was right. The office was with me because I had never cared. They liked to organize themselves. I took one project as proof and put Dumbo ears in charge. That way, when he looked good, it made me look good.

74

The Difference Is the Letter T

The boy and I braved the art world to look at art. I'd majored in painting as a freshman, though I couldn't paint, because I believed in an ideal self. I was always aware of the role of pain, the role of impossibility. I quit after a year to have a life. The boy seemed a natural at pain, carrying his mom in the balls of his fists. We were just getting to know each other. He stuffed his hands in his pockets and bit his tongue like a thumb. He looked at me as if for guidance. "Paint," I said, ready to lecture. He repeated me, his small voice lost in time, like back from a future where my speech had long deteriorated. Maybe, I thought, he knew enough already. He had drawn his family line to me through some deft reckoning, a bastard's understanding of fatherhood.

The Smell Was Asian

A familiar smell filled me up when I entered. I almost
looked for my parents. I hoped I wasn't attracted to her
because of childhood. In our apartment, the wifely woman and I never cooked, so we never scared away all those
years between now and repression. The Asian girl wore
an apron I got off in a hurry. She let the kimchi burn.

My Therapist Had a Name for It

Afterward, she panted like she'd done most of the work, and maybe I had let her; it had certainly *felt* like giving in. But it was a break I'd needed—wasn't that the point of an affair? I tried to pretend it was. I knew the point was more like the point of a knife, like I felt against the wall of my conscience. I had always been chicken.

Fame

My excuse had been a movie, alone, so now I had to make up a plot. The wifely woman never went to the movies without me, anyway. I was the one, she said, who wanted to escape my life. I said I'd seen Brad Pitt go crazy but it was nothing new. The first crazy was always the truest. After that, the actors only mimicked themselves.

Inheritance, Non-genetic #1

So I got the job, and for getting it I inherited a stack of papers one could call an office. I had no clue the color of the floor, I mean. For a mess of a man, I hated clutter. My first week was a literal wash. I let the boy come in once his school let out, and he shredded like he could kill the past. I liked what it said about him, how he weathered the stares from coworkers who knew I'd never mentioned a son. His existence spat on the existence of the past.

Inheritance, Non-genetic #2

I paid the boy attention for the space he cleared, impressed by this silent exposure. I couldn't get his mom out of my head—in the hospital, she'd been dirty with death. But maybe that was why he tidied with a vengeance. I imagined Bruce Lee kicking the stacks of papers, exploding them on impact. The boy did one better. He put them in their place, like a movie about redemption. I was surprised by the sway of cleanliness, though I knew Christians who swore their showers on God.

He Put the Trash in My Hand

In the end, the boy crabbed a condom wrapper from the cracks of the couch. The wifely woman used birth control. I hadn't let the white girl over since the boy appeared, pointing a genetic arrow. Now he pinched the wrapper as if contemplating his birth, though this was a projection— he was five and couldn't know what he was holding. I tried to blank my face on the topic of procreation. I said, "You sure are a detective for trash." I said, "I bet you a buck per scrap." I opened my wallet and realized what I was missing. He was holding my emergency. In back corners, he found: a bottle cap, two pencils, and cat fur. I followed him, counting our oversights. The wifely woman would be spared. I paid the boy in Honest Abe, showing, by a trick, how I could make a fiver a bowtie.

81

When in Rome

Randy and I went to a Raiders game to remember losing. Or maybe because I wanted to lose in something I
wasn't playing. We watched the football scoot between
gladiators, waiting for a lion to snatch a leg. One of the
boys (they were boys now, younger than us) fell in a heap
and didn't rise. The crowd cheered. They were distracted from the score. They wanted bloodless blood. "We
could still win," Randy said. I said, "Not us." He said the
kid who'd gone down was important to the other team. I
hadn't been paying attention. The lion gnawed at my hip
and I thought, this is my one day off.

What I Meant When I Said Sold Out

Sometimes at work, I thought, what is the point of work?
Sometimes I thought this wasn't a symptom of work but
a symptom of being human. I bossed the office now. I
brought a cake to show I wasn't serious. "I didn't know,"
Dumbo ears said. "You mean business." I left it in the box
from the supermarket. I wanted this to say, I care about
you as far as buying and selling. As they ate, I ate my hate
out.

I Was Running out of Excuses

The white girl leased a Hummer to drive it by our house each dusk. The wifely woman grew scared. I knew who it was because the white girl sent texts as she went by. I kept my phone on silent and the boy inside. She'd been having some sort of crisis ever since she found out about him, though I didn't see what difference a child made on top of never. I had told her the wifely woman was wifely. The white girl zoomed past the house and texted she'd bought a second cat—so she could have one more than me. "I bought a new dining table," she texted. "I'm re-doing my bathroom." I wondered where the money was coming from and then what it meant that she had stopped saving for the future. I grew scared in those moments, too. She texted that she'd bought the TV I'd ogled once in a catalog she'd left in the bathroom. I didn't know what to say. I erased the texts. I smiled at the wifely woman with a shaky understanding of the white girl's rage.

Illegitimate or Otherwise

We brought the boy to show my parents his permanence.
I'd done the same with the wifely woman three years before, and still did, but I thought it might work this time. My
dad had once hinted at grandkids. They lived on the far
side of the city, in a suburb of their own, overlooking the
sea. I remembered the shithole I'd grown up in, before
Dad stopped cooking and expanded outside Koreatown,
when all the alcohol made a bigger dent. Who would have
thought white people would eat sushi rolls with no sushi
in it? Though I knew better than to call it sushi—it was
kimbap—even if the menu said sushi. Being Korean was
like that. The boy had probably lived unsushi sushi since
his mother died. By which I mean, what do you call that?
When the world isn't ready to call something what it is?
My mother gave the boy money when he bowed. I had
taught him to bow like a Korean, until his back hurt.

85

Part of My Problem Was Ownership

My therapist had moved, uprooted the roots of others. I couldn't help but think: me, *The Other*. In my head, I was a movie. I peeked into her office, past the new therapist, who didn't realize where she was standing. All I wanted today was help. The doctor was out. I had to stop myself from pointing at our carpet stain.

A Question Answered

I never guessed until it happened that it would be the Asian girl, or how relieved I'd be even as I watched her scuttle my love boat. The wifely woman just stood there at first; then she eased the boy behind her back as if afraid the girl would attack him. Maybe she was afraid the girl would see he was half-white, and the three of us all yellow. I felt the anticipation, a nervous smile. I hid my irresponsible joy behind putting together the boy's Lego car. We'd been working at it together for what felt as long as an adolescence—he kept looking at me like how could I, an adult, be confused by a five-year-old's toy? I'd thrown away the instructions because I'd wanted him to be creative. The wifely woman fluttered her hand and said she knew I wasn't faithful, but she wished I had better taste. This seemed to hurt the Asian girl more than anything I had imagined said, but maybe what hurt her was that the wifely woman was Asian, too, and prettier. I nearly felt as if I could walk away, as if the fight was between them; I nearly felt a joke coming. The wifely woman dug her heel into my toe—it would be black for a remorseless month. I jumped up holding my foot, brimming over with happiness. I knew how painless my toe would be if we had dispossessed each other.

A Promotion by Any Other Name

I called my distraction delegation, and they liked that. Nobody wanted me hanging over them. Only Dumbo ears eyed me for a screw up. I was too busy with my screw ups at home to screw up work. When you let money go, I learned, it went on being money. Not so with life. A surprise son should have been enough of a warning to stop cheating. But I had cheated for numbness, to get to where I could stop caring, and then I had cared whether the wifely woman cared if I could stop. I was afraid now that she was giving me a last chance. I needed a forever of chances, or I needed a chance to last forever. I was too old to start a habit of success. Even Dumbo ears knew that.

The Heart Has a Waiting Room

The wifely woman said what she was doing with me was trying to give in without giving up. I had thought I would be prepared, if she left me. Now I wished I were a praying man. On the weekend, I found a liquor store that delivered. I opened my emergency meds. I saw the date but didn't care. The pills still worked, which I tried telling her. They didn't care if they expired.

What Children Know

I taught the boy football, trying to avoid the wifely woman's anger. He was good at catch, bad at throw; I had to stop myself from petting his head like a dog. My love of sanctioned violence confused him. I could sense him sensing the contradiction as he tackled me. The bigger man, I'd told him after another boy stepped on his sandcastle; he'd carried home the teary mud as proof. Our Little CSI, the wifely woman had said, maybe remembering his old obsession with death. In the yard, he went at me like I'd mugged him, like he'd found me later on a park bench, availed of the weapon I'd threatened him with. The wifely woman cheered my take-down. But he couldn't hurt me— he was only five and wasn't hers.

90

Kindergarten Doesn't Have Detention

My mother called to recommend a book she thought would fill some hole in my life. I thought maybe she'd come around on the boy; Dad was a drinker for lack of grandkids. They never gave up on me leaving the wifely woman for someone Korean and desperate for children. The book trumpeted Korean mothering, part of a new fad that had started with the Chinese. The wifely woman looked over my shoulder as I wrote down the title, then took the pencil from me and drew a Chinese emoticon, something implying oppression. She was a genius at emoticons; I thought she must make them up. I didn't want to talk about the boy's latest terrorizing, especially with the wifely woman there, but I also did. "How did you ever handle me?" I asked my mother. "I was a bad kid, wasn't I?" She said to read the book. I wondered when she'd graduated from criticism to avoidance—her silence was so unusual I realized she'd hung up. "The boy will be okay," the wifely woman said. I wondered if my mother had known what I was saying as well. I wondered if she'd wanted to talk to him.

91

Can You Adopt a Grandkid?

Or maybe my mom's main problem with the boy was that she missed babies. The boy had shown up too big for booties and unconditional love. The last decade, I knew, she'd felt empty. "Would you want," I asked on the phone, "to make the boy his first kimbap?" Her love had always started in the stomach. She said, "Do you feel trapped? Is that what you're asking me?" I wrung the phone around its waist. I said how could I *ask* her about what *I* felt, didn't she mean say? She was always saying. I got ready to hang up, saddling a sigh. But then she said, "Well, you ever need a babysitter," a question like a statement.

Onward

I made the mistake of messaging Randy, that prince of the insensitive. He said sowing seeds was a matter of nature; alimony had left him broke. He said, leave no records, while texting. He said, even if it was too late it wasn't too late. He said, but sometimes it was too late. He asked if she was prettier. When I said no, he said then what did he know, as if that settled it. I got it into my head that I had to visit the remaining girl, the white one, to see if *she* was prettier—I couldn't remember. I realized I was saving her for *just in case*. At the white girl's apartment, I saw all the new things she'd bought after I made it clear we would never buy them together. Her eyes dropped to my hips. She was pretty enough. I loathed myself as I counted the money she'd wasted. I noticed she'd already gotten rid of her cats.

Instinct Was Dead
for Valentine's Day

The wifely woman made her storms in the background; her stare never teetered between attack and retreat. I tried to hold that gaze, like in an animal encounter. But I was the flip-flopper. I was the wild. She was human; given time, she might forgive and forget. Either way, it would be a decision.

The Little Black Book

It didn't take long before I hated myself again. When I called, the white girl was getting over a cold. Her voice scratched through the phone wires. I said I didn't mind catching it, picturing a future of me and the wifely woman and the boy trading coughs. The white girl said she hadn't asked. I thought it might be nice for a while to be too sick to leave the house.

At Least I Felt Bad Afterward

I said I wouldn't meet her but we knew I would. It took a lot out of me to be nice and I needed to stock up on mistakes. "I got rid of everything," the white girl said when I arrived. It was true her apartment was empty. I wondered if she was leaving, if this was goodbye. I would stop sabotaging myself. She said, "I want you to sit in the middle. I want you to be furniture." I had nothing to leave in that apartment but myself.

I'm Not Saying, I'm Just Saying

The boy watched me pack equipment he'd never seen before: poles and long thin boards with boots and Eskimo clothes from the garage. Was I a mystery to him? I was taking a trip to reconnect with boys' nights, which I'd missed since he, *the* boy, had dropped into my life and claimed genes. Or maybe I was leaving because the wifely woman needed time off from me. "You were supposed to wait until night," she said now, like this was a matter for Santa Claus. "Can't you see he wants to go, too?" I pictured the drinking game where, on our last morning, after tallying our race times, the slowest drunk skier skied naked. And I would take the boy? I almost looked forward to the shameless shame and the spray stinging me alive; I knew I was badly out of practice. How could I say, "I want to get away from you?" They looked at me like I'd already said it.

Black Diamond

I stood on the slope distracted by white. Clouds clumped, and still I wore sunglasses. Nature was blinding. I wanted it to blind me. One step over, Randy unscrewed his flask, tasting freedom, perhaps, for the first time since his jail stint. I breathed up all that speed ahead of me, holding it in. Randy laughed and started down; suddenly I wanted to trip him. I wanted to pity him sincerely. I wanted to blame the alcohol, and then I wanted to come clean and be forgiven.

98

The Boy Never Stopped Calling Jerry, "Tom"

In the end, the poor cat got it. I came home from a machine-like work day, feeling magnanimous, thinking the time right to win back the wifely woman, and found the cat splayed out, unable to walk. The boy had wishboned its legs. "Tom won't stand up," he said, master of the obvious, captain of cruel. I ignored him, afraid to recognize myself in either his deed or denial. This went past acting out; the cat tried to drag its hind parts across the hardwood. I rooted for it to sink its little claws into the boy, knowing we'd have to put it down, wishing it one manageable revenge. The cat had learned to like the boy; it hadn't seen this coming. I remembered them chasing its tail together. I couldn't discipline the boy without wanting to injure him—I waited for the wifely woman. When she got home, she locked the boy in his room and us in ours. "We have to stop fighting," she said.

It Was a Large Enough World
When It Needed to Be

The wifely woman had been a beauty and then a hungry teen and then a beauty again. I had caught her with a bout of flattery, following a string of secret restaurants I had accumulated over a decade in the city. There wasn't much choice for her in the suburbs. She said she lived the entire world on her trips, so when she came back, she could stand a little cooping up. "You could always run away," I said once. She flipped a coin, but she was in Germany then so I didn't see how it landed.

100

I Could Feel His Pulse

I took the boy to the pet shop to remind him about vulnerability. You would think, since his mother was dead and he'd just found me . . . but he was a child and had a child's memory. It had been two weeks since he'd crippled the cat; when we put it down, he was still waiting for it to pop up again. He was still waiting. I was still waiting. I wanted him to know what he'd done, the permanence, but the wifely woman protested. He must have known somewhere inside of him. In the pet shop, I thought about the ways the boy could hurt the animals. This is my son, I thought. I wasn't ready for him to have another pet; the last one had been mine. "Is Jerry here?" he asked. He closed his hand over my thumb.

I Didn't Know How to Parent

I took the boy to the top of a building to look down over the city. To know we could look down. He said he felt like he could blow away in the wind. I waited for more, but he was speaking literally. There was no meaning except to take his hand.

102

Ode to Dumbo Ears

Dumbo ears, oh, Dumbo ears. You counted my hours and spent your lunches charting how much I worked. I can't say I didn't know you had it in you. I couldn't even argue inaccuracy. I argued hey, what a stalker. I argued, Benedict Arnold. But the big boss was little with liquor. Dumbo ears, you learned. Betrayed by a bottle of bourbon. Your car, when you find it—you know my work. You don't know the story of the man who cried sheep? The wolf ate him, too. The wolf eats everyone.

Don't Call Me Yellow

I collapsed on the couch, thinking about the work I didn't have anymore. It was a superb couch. I'd thought I would be happy. The wifely woman earned enough for us both, and the boy, but I was the boy's father—was that it? I knew what my mother would say: she had escaped a war, found work in a country that cursed her skin color. They even called cowardice after it, or maybe that was a miscategorization of hue. When the wifely woman came home, I was still moping. The boy ran face-first into the couch when I shifted my legs. He had no sense of shame or pride. I watched him down there on the floor, his arms still churning for a hug. And I thought, I feel responsible for that? It was my sperm. I had to get a job I loved, one that wasn't about shame or pride.

Epic Fights

After five years of silence, five years of talk. I looked up
distraught in the thesaurus. The wifely woman kept at-
tacking herself. What was I if she was *stupid, gullible,
blind*? Odysseus spearing poor Cyclops, who was only
who he'd been made? The wifely woman wove a tapes-
try. I fucked Calypso. I studied my affair in the threads.
Unwind this, she said. Night after night, I felt the fragility
of her creation. I told myself the past was not the future.

A Black Eye Is Nothing

We had an excuse—not in front of the boy—though she wasn't beholden by genes. He had come into our lives out of nowhere. Later, I touched a tiny fist-print in the wall, then went looking for him, to adjust his understanding of fault.

You Say Hello, I Say Goodbye

The wifely woman said I had to get out of the house. I still didn't have a new job. She said to take the boy on a trip. She said she was working herself up to forgiveness—being alone was her test. I took the boy to L.A. since he barely knew he was Korean. His mother, before she died, had taught him only whiteness. Now we bloated our bellies with bo ssam—he liked the little shrimp; he was always looking for life in miniature. "How big is Korea?" he asked. I told him it was sized to slip through the cracks; I had. We went to a noraebang and I sang a whine over the wah-wah, letting him pick the song. I wasn't ready to go home.

Sentimentality

When we got back, the wifely woman said, "You said just a day." I said, "Just say you missed me." It hadn't been my plan, but I could see the weakness in her eyes. The boy skipped past her, singing nonsense karaoke. I believed the trip had taught him something about his origin. The wifely woman pecked my cheek, and I could feel the heat hiding inside her. The boy said, "Korea is in The Angeles." I patted his chest, hoping he would get the message.

Tom

We agreed that the boy should get a second chance. Or she agreed and I understood that she loved me again. Could love replace a murdered pet? I looked at kittens online. I wanted to keep the boy away from pets until I believed his repentance. He pointed at each jpg and said, "That one." I thought, wait for the one he doesn't like. He had liked Jerry, and he had treated Jerry like a science experiment. In bed, while I was still tender, the wifely woman said, "He needs to know we don't blame him." I thought, once a tiger tastes man. Once a man tastes tiger. But I wanted a kitten, too. I missed that silent reliance, noiseless until the purr in your lap. The Scottish fold seemed to frighten the boy, its ears limp, as if broken. "That one," I told the wifely woman.

How to Buy Life

We went to visit the cat on the farm to see it in another unnatural environment. Then we were supposed to know how it would adjust. I looked at the boy and wondered what he was thinking, if he remembered his birth. Flowers grew along the edges of the porch and the first we saw of the cat was her claws. She reached out from the dark to kill something bright, and I thought, good, we needed a survivor.

Let Someone Else Drive

I liked to leave the windows down—it had been a long winter—but the kitten kept climbing the boy's shirt, batting at the wind through the crack. I wanted to warn it, to explain that the boy could be a killer. I wanted to bring it home and let it dig up our old cat, as the boy watched. I wanted everyone to love each other. My feelings were complicated. I knew this was the point in the novel where the protagonist is revealed to the reader by an object. Where, if you pay close enough attention, you know the protagonist has changed before he does. But all I could think to do was hand the wheel to the wifely woman and reach back for the scruff on the kitten's neck.

Forgiveness

She made us listen to "Thriller" every time we made up; I didn't know what it meant to her. We danced our way through loving each other again. I liked Michael Jackson, but at first I couldn't stop thinking, *zombies*. Then her smooth body, like the dip of a buoy, made me remember the living. "Don't ever do it again," she said. Michael Jackson was dead.

How Can I Explain This?

At last, I wanted a career—I'd passed thirty, I had an illegitimate child, I cohabitated—I couldn't believe my parents had been right about me. My generation was overly qualified, underly ambitious. I recalled a Christmas flick about a mouse who doubts the person of Santa Claus. "All of us," he signs an editorial. But that's a movie. In real life, there could be no appealing the world. I tore up the classifieds as soon as I read them. The jobs were like a network of underwater caves: you dove down and hoped for a pocket of air. I called Randy to commiserate. We got fired from a bar. In the morning, I was supposed to take the boy to school, and he awoke my hangover. "You *smell* like no job," the boy said. He didn't grasp the plight of the worker. He bossed me into the shower. After I dropped him off, I went to the drug store to tear up another paper. The wifely woman had made circles in mine, and I was still above taking suggestions.

Kindergarten Report Cards

The boy brought home judgment. Five seemed too young to be good or bad. It made me protective of his potential. I felt like a father. The wifely woman tore open the envelope. Momentum seemed shifting within. He had passed into our home; he had passed a blood test; he was getting adoption papers. But smart enough, socialized enough? We'd been called in before: talking back, excessive. We'd evaluated ourselves. I wanted to tell him to forget *years*, but there was a strict passage of development. The wifely woman shook the letter like salt. "It's just words," she said, as if numbers would hurt more. They would have. The boy was just normal. But it was all subjective.

Which One Is a Bull Market?

I wanted to start a business, I just didn't know in what. I was tired of looking for a job. The world seemed open to me then. The wifely woman made money. I asked myself what I knew. I knew what sold things, or what people thought sold them—the difference between commission and salary—I'd never really earned what I'd earned. I knew plenty about self-loathing. I told the wifely woman the first step was admitting my problem. She said, "You've always been a success at quitting." She said, "It doesn't work if you stage your own intervention." I said, "I didn't quit I was fired."

Into That Good Night

I picked a floundering product as a point of pride. Ads were a type of death. Progress seemed designing book covers. Books were already goners, or so writers kept writing. I could help them go gently. I jinxed the business before it began, celebrating at a pub. People there were full of intentions. Randy had the idea to get the jinx out of the way first. "Everyone gets ruined," he said, "at some point." The wifely woman set a curfew. At midnight, I was in pajamas, designing drunk. I practiced on the books I knew—*The Moderate Gatsby, In the Heart of the Armpit of the Country*. But as I clothed them, I didn't want them to die. Before, I'd undressed their words like anyone else, craving nakedness. Now I shook off my skin and covered them. The night was young and full of ways to hate myself.

Howls

The boy was a reminderer. Or maybe he thought we didn't know his birthday since we weren't there for his birth. At first, I hadn't known. The wifely woman had gotten it out of him. Wanting, the wifely woman said, was a good sign. She said it like he was a feral child. Usually I was the one to underestimate him, or to throw him to the wolves.

Don't Feed the Animals

I tried to remember telling the white girl about the zoo; I was sure I hadn't. Against all evidence, I didn't believe in self-sabotage. In fact, the wifely woman was in New York, PR-ing a rise to fame or a meltdown—I hadn't listened closely. It was always one or the other, and didn't matter which. I wondered if the boy remembered the white girl from that first day, just before his mother died, when he'd surprised me with his genes. The white girl was shameless—and what good was a mistress, if not for shame? She rustled the boy's hair like a bird's nest, like when her hand lifted he was missing eggs. The boy watched the lions chew each other's ears, pretending peace. "Like Tom," he said. Our new kitten. I watched the white girl's eyes register this ignorance. She thought she knew everything, since here was the boy. She plucked a flower as she walked behind us, then tucked it into her hair. April was indeed cruel to her. In Korea, only crazy women wore flowers in their hair. The boy studied me as we passed the giraffes. I thought: steel walls. I thought: cages. It was strange how he could already see through me. He tapped the white girl on the hip, and when she bent down, he snatched the flower and held it through the fence for a calf to nibble, its body juggling on its flimsy legs.

A Glimpse of the Future

The boy wanted to make a zoo in our yard. He safaried the streets and came back skunk-sprayed. We had watched cartoons of Pepé Le Pew—I'd thought he would know the difference. The stink got in the house before we could go out for tomato juice. We used spaghetti sauce and ketchup. "Why?" the wifely woman asked as we scrubbed him. He said *I* had been happy at the zoo. But I'd been miserable. He said we met a woman there like his mother. But the two were nothing alike, only white, and the suburbs abounded with white women. So he was projecting, I thought. This was the first he'd mentioned his mother since her death, and the wifely woman looked suspicious. Her nose rolled up like a window shade, though it could have been from the smell. The boy reeked of innocence.

119

How to Give Birth to a Five-Year-Old

It was just a chick flick, but the boy was supposed to be in bed. So even Matthew McConaughey woke up a sense of our old lives. "Nine months he's been with us," the wifely woman said. "He's ready to be born." He had impregnated our privacy. I said, "Push." I said, "Breathe." I was getting into it. The acting was so bad it was good. She kicked the blanket off the couch and I thought about her without him. I thought about when we didn't know I had a son. Then I stopped thinking. When I saw him on the stairs and my brain turned on again, my first reaction was, don't let *her* see. My second was, which of us was he crying for?

People Wondered About the Boy at
the Release Party

I Photoshopped the boy on the cover, a triumph of white-washing. You couldn't even tell he was half-Korean. The design made a lot of money. I didn't know why I was so proud of it. He was proud. We called it *his* book—kindergarten had taught him possession. I didn't know the author. The wifely woman knew what I'd done but didn't say anything. She let it be a victory. She let me turn it into a loss myself. When I realized what I'd sold away, she was there to comfort me.

Banned

The party slumped off the hook and to the floor. Randy passed out in the bathroom. The bar put a photo of him on the door—an *un*wanted sign. I suffered from association, a suburban hangover. The drive back from the city, Randy told me, while the sun insisted morning, sobered him to a worse sickness. The ill that got to us all—that longing for the mess of civilization, a mess we could never mess up. In the suburbs, our faults wore us; we were on the outside. I held the book I'd designed between two disdainful fingers, and slipped off the dust cover, leaving protection behind.

And After the End Came the End

I sought to take her out to assuage her memory, though it was true her memory could guide her. I had hurt her. I wondered if she would disappear again. In the past, I had let her, but now I was sure she loved me. I took her to a Woody Allen movie. Halfway through the Jewish part, the theater went up in smoke. "You call this avant garde?" I said. Someone else said, "Fire." Outside, I couldn't help wanting my money back, though I knew it wasn't worth it. I saw a ticket taker, objective correlative. The wifely woman cut me off. "You call that avant garde?" she asked the girl. That was what I loved about her—I still believed she could stop me from my own stupidity. We laughed until she said, "You call this a date?"

123

Sometimes the Boy Humped Her Leg Like a Dog

The thing is, they shouldn't call parent-teacher conferences *conferences*. The boy wasn't doing so badly for the
new kid; it was just that he'd been an angel before. I figured this change was him fitting in. "I try to put up with
all the death death death," his teacher said. I pointed out
this was after his mom died. She covered her mouth but
I knew she was only waiting an appropriate time. I waited
for her to ask about problems at home; I watched TV.
She'd said he was yanking girls' hair a little more than was
usual. What did she expect me to say? I had a bag full of
hair at home, and I wouldn't share? But she went on, and
went on, until I couldn't defend myself. Until I could only
stare at her shin and wonder what the boy loved.

Flying Reptiles

I dropped the boy at school, then spent the morning Photoshopping pterodactyls. The book: *Wings of Inefficiency*. For lunch, I drove into the city to surprise the wifely woman. She canceled a meeting I'd forgotten. I swallowed deeply, choking with guilt, but she ordered dessert. I insisted my card, though I never battled over breadwinning. She saw me every day, and *still* she lingered. I think I understood something. "Why don't we get married?" she whispered as I signed. I didn't know how to answer. I left my name in a flourish. When I got home, though, I messaged the white girl, "We have to save ourselves." I meant to marry. After she left, I still meant to marry. I tried to see the pterodactyls as birds. Then I remembered the boy. The wifely woman brought him home. She didn't ask again.

125

The Power of Invisible Molecules

I taught the boy the proper way to launch a kite: to let
the wind do the work. I told him the air had a weight of
its own. But when he took the string, he dragged the kite
behind him like a fish he could force to swim the sky. Far
away, it was easy to imagine him as someone else's kid.
Whose failures did not reflect mine. I told myself to wait.
At least long enough for him to circle back, until I could
make him see how the kite became its own animal, if giv-
en the chance; long enough for the differences between us
to be clear to us both.

What's the Point of Birthday Wishes?

Of course we got the boy what he wanted. I owed him a material life. I hadn't been there until his mom died—she had given him her soul. I tied a simple bow around the bike, but the wifely woman said it had to *seem* a surprise. He had to think we were going to let him down? I wondered. She said, "Boys like surprises," but I wasn't sure, being a boy myself. The only way to get a box big enough was to buy one. And then what else would he think it was? Though maybe that solved our problem—what the wifely woman really wished for him, I saw at last, was fulfillment. One expectation he could open up and accept.

127

I Had Trouble with Comparisons

The boy brought home an open carton and set it on the kitchen table like it meant something. I sorted through looking for worth. A few new dinosaur toys, a salamander tail (real), two self-moving Matchbox cars, and, most strangely, nine fingernails I hoped were false. I didn't want to touch them to tell. I still wouldn't know where they'd come from. They were painted pink, and their public display baffled me. Had he left them for me, or the wifely woman? I waited for him to come out of his room, not wanting to interrupt whatever he had to keep private. He stepped out in his "best" shirt, all black except for a white line down the middle. He called this his tie—I had tried to give him a real tie but he hated anything around his neck. I asked him, "Another tail?" to warm him up, thinking about our dead cat. He said, "Dad," with a tremble, and I realized at once that he was trying me out, "this is my apology box." I had no idea whether to hug him or seek a hug for myself, or seek help. I said, "And the nails?" He held one out to me. I was a biter. He hung his head and the *Dad* seemed to retreat into his mouth. "I'm sorry," he said, I didn't know why. I thanked God the nail felt false.

128

For the Record, I was Never Fooled

I went to pick up the cake thinking about the boy's two sad friends and two sad moms who didn't want to be there but sacrificed. I'd left the wifely woman with them. It was a party. She had no obligation to the boy, at least legal. But her motherly potential! The boy could see it, too, you could tell. He let her dress him. On the drive, the windshield was covered with pollen. The cake decoration contained ninjas with bleeding swords, the victims outside the frame. The two friends would like that; we had let the boy be boy. The mothers were beside the question, or out of the point. On the cake, sixth was spelled *sexth*. I glared at the teenagers behind the counter. "A bit obvious," I said, but I was late. I decided against trick candles.

129

Birthdays Are Overrated

Afterward, the boy kept holding up his hand and looking at it like his fingers webbed. I didn't want to know what deformation he saw—but I also did. I had always obsessed over deformations. I remembered Star Trek with my father, searching mirrors after my first Klingon, afraid the ridges would appear one day and never leave. That was what I had thought growing up was. Something sudden and impossible to take back. The boy, too, was thinking about age. He didn't know how to count six. He could no longer raise one hand as an answer. From then on five was a question.

130

A Second Chance at Kites

The boy's first bike ride, I felt an awareness of absence.
I tried to fit years in a day. I put the training wheels on, I
took them off, he fell bad but clung. This seemed to say:
we could succeed. My own childhood was still pending
results. I drove him back to the park where the kite-flyers
made kids laugh and cry. I let him bike the kite into the
air. Then I licked my finger to teach how to touch the
wind, how the world moved while we stood still. I held
my hands over his on the kite with the wind in our faces.
Finally I took a shot at showing him what it meant to stay.

It's Not My Fault, Is it?

I saw Randy in Shaw's swapping out large eggs for extra large. I tried to turn before he saw me, too, with the boy. "Who's this?" he asked. I said, "You save what, forty cents?" This was the suburbs. But I could see he was thinking the same: the burbs. I didn't know how to explain: he was my best friend but the boy was my best secret. I hadn't even known he existed until recently. "I'm six?" the boy kept saying, hardly believing himself. He seemed relieved he'd lived another year. He was a scared little boy. "Chickens come out of those," he said. Randy said, "Not out of these. Chickens lay two types of eggs. These don't have any babies in them." The boy started to cry. He was inconsolable.

An Idyll

The wifely woman and I took the boy to see his dead mom's favorite place: an ice cream factory built to look like a cow. I felt eager to go inside—the heat stuck to our skin. I pictured the variety of flavors. The wifely woman knelt and talked about cow stomachs, the four parts—none of which, the boy pointed out, was ice cream. Yet like everything, he absorbed what he heard. I realized she was talking about stages. Did he miss his past? I wondered what he would have been like if we had had his first five years. "Time to taste test," I said, but he shook his head. Suddenly, he didn't want to taste. My dad had always said if I ate lying down, I would turn into a cow. I had always said, then I would be holy.

They Call Time "Father"

And then finally it was summer again and the remnants of shells shimmered on the sand. When they washed up, something had died inside of them. I remembered the last summer, when the boy was sadder and happier. He was evener now, we hoped. He was six and his mother's death was a sixth of his life ago. He followed the wifely woman into the water. She picked up a shell and he picked up a shell behind her. This was his latest habit, which I thought kids grew out of earlier. I lay on the beach wanting to shut my eyes on his mimicking but not shutting them. I didn't know how the wifely woman had gotten such a grasp of him. She put her shell to her ear. He put his to his ear. But they were just clams. Later the two of them came back wet and dripped on me and the wifely woman teased me for being dry. The boy didn't seem to know why he was dripping, or how to make himself stop.

Acknowledgements

This book would not exist, would never have been written, really, if not for the encouragement from David Erlewine, Ronnie Scott, and Michael Seidlinger.

Thank you also to the CCM team, including Michael, Gabe Cardona, and Kyle Muntz.

Thank you to the editors at the following magazines, which published pieces of *I'm Not Saying, I'm Just Saying*: David at *JMWW*, Dawn Raffel at *The Literarian*, Meg Pokrass at *Blip*, Steve McDermott at *Storyglossia*, Ronnie at *The Lifted Brow*, Jarred McGinnis at *Beat the Dust*, Kirby Johnson and Sophie Rosenblum at *NANO Fiction*, Jane Wong at *Everyday Genius*, Lauren Becker at *Corium*, Brandon Hobson at *elimae*, Joel Smith at *Spork*, Jamie Iredell at *Atticus Review*, Lily Hoang at *Puerto del Sol*, Matt Bell at *The Collagist*, Karissa Chen at *Hyphen*, Scott Garson at *Wigleaf*, Caitlin Hayes at *Salt Hill*, Cheryl Olsen at *We Wanted to Be Writers*, Gina Frangello at *The Nervous Breakdown*.

Thank you to Cathy Chung, Kathy Fish, Matt Bell, Aimee Phan, and Marie Myung-Ok Lee for their very kind blurbs, each of which made me blush, and to Roxane Gay, who always always brings it.

Thank you to everyone who helped spread word of this book, and to those who offered their creativity and time for the "Romantics" month at *Sundog Lit*, all of who are dear to my heart and much admired, and with special thanks to Justin Daugherty.

Thank you to Vladimir Kapustin, whose beautiful cover image inspired me long before it graced this book.

Thank you to my friends, who encourage all of the writing I do, and to my family, who put up with all of the writing I do.

Nothing would matter, none of this narrative, or mine, without my wife, Ok Kyung Na, who I am realizing more and more is the start of my story, and our daughter, Grace Eun Chung, who is the start of a new story.

Thank you for reading.

Matthew Salesses was adopted from Korea at age two. He married a Korean woman, became a father, and writes about his family in a column for *The Good Men Project*. His essays and fiction have appeared in *The New York Times* Motherlode blog, *Glimmer Train*, *The Rumpus*, *American Short Fiction*, *Hyphen Magazine*, *Koream*, *Witness*, and others. He also wrote a novella, *The Last Repatriate*, and the chapbooks, *Our Island of Epidemics* and *We Will Take What We Can Get*.

CPSIA information can be obtained
at www.ICGtesting.com
Printed in the USA
LVOW04s1703040116

469054LV00024B/2046/P